A Darker Shadow

2

THE KNOCKER

By AD Bane

A Darker Shadow: The Knocker
Copyright © 2018 AD Bane

Published by
AD Bane Publishing
British Columbia, Canada
Published in Canada, Printed in the USA
First Printing, 2018

ISBN-13: 978-0991833023
ISBN-10: 0991833023

To obtain additional copies of this book you can find it available at Amazon. If you like it buy it. Help support a struggling author!

Visit ADBane.com/news to keep up to date with everything Mr. Bane is currently working on.

FOR THE BROKEN,
AND THE WANDERER

A Darker Shadow

Look for these other chapters coming soon!

FOREWORD

When I wrote *The Darkness Within* I didn't really have any intention of continuing the arc. I just wanted to try my hand at writing a story about a tormented exorcist. I really liked the idea of a man so troubled by the demons of his past he can barely manage life, and yet he has these powers that make him almost super-human. It's so relatable, and yet so foreign. But it was the reader demand that made me keep going. Everyone I gave the first chapter to said they liked it and I should write more.

Continuing a story that has no real direction isn't easy. That's why TV series so often start off feeling like each episode is a story of its own, where superman has one person to save and that's it. Show over. Wrap it up, go home. When I wrote *The Knocker* I knew I wanted this to become a series that would keep going on, but I didn't know how far it would go. I tried to keep it simple and to the point, and I was open to the possibility that this might be Michael's only moment in the light. I tried to build the character without building the story. Thankfully it wasn't the end and Michael lived another day to fight another demon. And it was here in the pages of a four thousand word sequel that the character started to take shape.

Michael started to find himself.

Greater in battle than the man who would conquer a thousand-thousand men, is he who would conquer just one — himself.

- Dhammapada v 104-105

"How many rooms upstairs?" he asked.

She replied, "Three: two on the left, one on the right."

"And at the end of the hall?" he asked.

"Just three," she said.

Then what had made its home there and hidden itself beneath her eyes?

THE STORY SO FAR

She knew something was wrong with her daughter. She knew she needed help. But it was hard to find someone who'd take her seriously and harder still to find someone who knew how to perform an exorcism. That was why she called him.

Before the exorcist, a priest had come by from the local parish. The church sometimes did exorcisms, he'd said, but they had to assess the situation, decide whether or not it really was a demon. Times now gone, exorcisms had been more common place and they'd done hundreds all over the world. But these days people are generally just crazy, not possessed. Still, Miss Vasquez knew it was fear in his eyes when he saw Nikki huddled against the wall beneath the window. She could tell the old priest knew as well as she did there was something in the closet looking back.

But his diagnosis wasn't helpful. "Take her to a doctor," he said. "She's very ill."

But she hadn't. The wise men of medical science couldn't help her daughter now. Only someone who knew what was hiding inside the shadows of her downtown apartment could save them.

She never could remember where she'd gotten his number from. She dug it from the bottom of her purse, hastily scribbled on a piece of card. The name was easy. Of course she knew who he was. The rogue warrior, despised by the church because he saw things they could never train their parishioners to see. And he had power over them.

They just called him Michael.

When he answered the phone she knew it was him. He had that same calm demeanor when Anna let him into the apartment kitchen. Only the man they'd told her about could be that calm. And as he walked into hell to save her child she felt his calm, too. It was contagious.

When it was done she'd rung his hand and hugged her Nikki as if she'd never let go. Michael had saved them, she knew. But as she watched him leave she wondered who would save him.

THE KNOCKER

The lights flickered for a moment. He watched as the golden life left their bulbs, draining away until their very last presence was a lingering shadow in his memory. It was so empty, that cold silence they left in their wake – empty and dreadfully chill. He could almost hear their voices, feel their touch on him. In the dark they came. In the dark the worlds collided and theirs became as much a part of his, though no one else could see it. Even now they weren't far, only just beyond his reach.

The dark lasted only a moment before the lights were alit again, his shadow cast in their dull radiance. It shone on the wet asphalt, on the rain and the water that ran in rivers through the gutters. It was a miserable thing, he thought: miserable, and yet he liked it. Even the cold was to be cherished for its own brutal ways. They hated it, and that was reason enough.

From his jacket he took a cigarette and lit it, retreating into the shadows at the edge of the street. For a time he only watched the embers drift away as the cigarette shrank before his eyes, not wanting to smoke it and yet knowing he would eventually. And if it burnt away to nothing before he did smoke it he would only light another. But why? He asked himself that so many times, but the answer was a mystery to him. Perhaps it would always be a mystery, a mystery why they called to his thoughts, a mystery why their wretched voices never ceased.

He could hear her footsteps in the rain even before she spoke. With each fall there was a splash that followed, for the street and the alley were choked with the rain: and it'd been raining since last week. She was pretty, he thought; certainly she must be. He could almost see her face through the darkness. She was so beautiful, so young and stunning. Her face and her smile would've forced back even the dark and the cold. And kind too, he thought. She smiled at him and there was something in her eyes, in her lips, and it made him trust her.

"Michael?" she asked, and her footfalls stopped in the street. "Are you Michael?"

He didn't turn to her. He didn't want to, didn't want to believe it. Certainly he must've been wrong. He hadn't seen her face. It was only his imagination, or what he'd hoped – a fools hope. How he hated to believe something so terrible could happen to one so kind. And yet his conscience told him to stop being naive. Yes, he was naive.

He still stayed in the shadows, drawing on the remnants of his cigarette and shaking away the ash. It was his fourth already today, he realized: too many too fast. They would kill him one day, if he hadn't done himself in already. It was inevitable.

Her voice returned to him as if from a long way off and through a very cold night. *Michael?*

"Yes," he said, and he stepped from the shadows to make himself known.

"Oh, thank God!" she replied. Goodness knew no one else deserved it.

She *was* pretty in her own way, he thought. Certainly not as he'd imagined, and yet there was that light in her eye, though clouded by darkness like the ache behind his own, a darkness he knew too well.

"When I spoke to you on the phone I wondered," she said, and her eyes moved away nervously.

"Who was it sent you again?" he asked.

"Adelina," she said, "gave me your card."

"Didn't know I—" But it was coming back to him: a hasty set of digits and a signature scribbled on box-card, and even now she handed it to him, the ink fading and the edges worn. It'd come a terrible long way to find itself once more in his hands.

"Keep it," he said. Then, "Did you know Nikki?" he asked. The silence enveloped his words. He wondered if he maybe shouldn't have said them because she was looking at him now with a tear rolling down her cheek.

"I did," she said. "We were close. We grew up together. Adelina is as a mother to me, ever since--"

"I'm sorry," he answered.

"I couldn't believe it when I heard it," she said. "I always thought Nikki was so happy." Her voice became distant and shaken. "I've missed her terribly."

"Is that why you called me?" he asked. "Because of her?"

For a moment confusion was evident on her face, but she broke it. "No, no," she said. "Not at all. It was Adelina who recommended you to me. She said you helped them when no one else could. She said you know about things, very dark things – these kinds of things."

He only looked at her and said nothing for a time, reading carefully the emotions that crossed her face. "I couldn't help Nikki," he said quietly at last. "Or maybe I did something wrong, I don't know now."

"Adelina said what happened to Nikki you couldn't help," she replied. "She didn't doubt you, Michael. Not for a moment."

It was little reassurance to him, but it was kindly meant, and he took it as such. It wasn't the doubt of others that troubled him.

He lit another cigarette and drew on it long, still watching the glowing embers. How they reminded him, how they recalled such terrible things as took hold of his sleepless nights, things as couldn't be forgot. That one place he'd only ever been once . . . he shook his head to clear them away.

The rain started falling again. He could feel it touching his face and hands in tiny prickles. The razor-rain was always bad in Baltimore these days he'd heard.

"How did it happen?" he asked at last. "Did she say?"

"Nikki?" asked the girl. "Put a gun in her mouth." Her words dry and empty. "Said she wouldn't go to hell, said they couldn't take her."

"Ironic," he replied thoughtfully.

"What?"

"That those should be her last words," he answered.

"Do you believe that?" she asked, "that she went to hell?"

He looked at her hard, thoughtful. "No," he replied. "Not for a moment. But Nikki did."

"I never understood why they believed," she said thoughtfully, as if to herself.

There was another silence that fell between them, he to his own dreadful remorse and she no doubt by the sadness in her eyes thinking of Nikki. He drew on his cigarette and watched the ash fall, vanishing into the wet asphalt. It'd been his fault, he thought. Nikki should've been alive; he should've gone back; he should've made sure. He should've known. He was naive. He was a fool.

The rain was falling steadily when she spoke again. Her words were shaken, though perhaps only with cold. "So, can you help me then?" she asked, her eyes on him, a grieving plea.

He returned her gaze. "I'll try," he replied with certainty. "But I'll need to know what's happening, and I'll need to see it--" He paused, words suddenly lost to him. What if she died too? What then? What would another failure do to him? "--the house," he finished, catching his breath.

"When can you come?" she asked, "to see it, I mean. How long are you going to be in Baltimore?"

"I leave in the morning for Liberty," he replied. "Work."

"So soon," she returned.

"Just passing through," he said. "Actually it's a wonder you caught me at all." He hadn't planned to stop in Baltimore. The anger he'd felt when he'd heard about Nikki would've driven him all the way to the north. He wanted solitude.

"When will you be returning?" she asked.

But he ignored her. The truth was he had no idea. "Tell me what's going on," he said instead.

Her eyes grew cold. Even in the dark he could see the shadows in them, and she shook. There was something dreadful in her face and her words were empty as one who frights at even the thought of what they must say. "At night I can feel it," she said. "Cold and empty. It watches me. It won't stop looking. It won't stop. Its eyes are watching, always watching, and they're terrible eyes, great and awful. And sometimes I can feel it cold, as a touch. Or sometimes there's sounds."

"Sounds?" he asked. They often made sounds that gave them away, like the fools that they are, thinking no one can hear them but themselves. "What kind?"

"Sounds in the night like a knock on the wall, like a scratch under the floor. Sometimes the curtains move, sometimes the doors will shut with a creak of hinges that never make a sound, even when all the windows are closed. And I can always feel it watching, always watching."

"How long?" he wondered. "How long has this been happening?"

"A week?" she said, uncertain. "Perhaps longer. Not before Nikki--" And her voice broke into a sob. "Oh God, is this what Nikki went through? This terrible horror?"

He said nothing. No it wasn't, not quite: for Nikki it'd been much worse. For Nikki the monster had haunted her every step and consumed her mind.

"I should see the house tonight," he said, his mind at last made up.

"Tonight?" she asked. "Can you?"

He paused for only a moment, himself in silent contemplation. But he'd already made up his mind. "Yes," he said. Yes, he had to.

"Oh, thank-you!" she cried, her words turning to sobs again. "It's dreadful lying awake at night listening to every noise in terror it might be closer than the last, or that it might be my name in the dark."

He nodded. He knew what that was like. "Take me there," he said.

The house was on Bradford, hid away amidst all the others that hardly looked any different. It wasn't a big house. There was no car in the alley, no lights were on, and the door was left only just ajar. She wasn't concerned of burglaries. She said as much when they stood before it. And who would dare to enter such a place, anyhow? When he stood in the street he could feel the darkness inside the house. He knew it was there watching, and yet she pushed the door open and went in without hesitation.

The cemented steps were worn, the paint on the rail faded: it gave way when he touched it, loosened from years of weathering beneath the rain and the sun – and even snow. And yet it wasn't so bad, he thought. Certainly he'd seen worse. It wasn't *so* uninviting, not at all somewhere he should've been loath to live himself.

The lights flickered when she turned the switch, painfully indecisive. But they came on, he noted, and that was good. But that momentary flash stayed behind his eyes for a moment, there to prey on the naivety of his sight. He saw them. They were there, betrayed by their shadows, watching him. They were not naive.

"Please make yourself comfortable," she said, and she smiled at him kindly, more kindly even than he'd imagined she could. "Can I get you anything?" she asked.

"Not me," he returned. "Do you have tea? Herbal."

"Mint."

"Then heat water," he said.

She went to the kitchen, vanishing around the corner, the cold and the empty silence in her wake. The air of that house was a deadly calm, and yet not so silent. He heard them even now – a scratch beneath the floor, a shuffle in the wall, a quiet whisper as the wind in the rafters. She was right, they watched her.

"Does anyone else know?" he asked.

"Know what?" she called in return.

"About this. *It.*"

"Yes," she replied.

"Who?"

"The priest, Father Cautting. When it first happened I spoke to him. That's why I'm so glad you agreed to meet me. No one else would, you see."

"Why?" he asked.

"The priest--" Her words failed her again, but it was only a moment before she regained herself. "He came here. He was concerned. But he wouldn't come in. He only stood on the step and spoke to me. He was worried, he said, and he wanted to help me. And I asked him to come in, but he said *It* wouldn't like that.

There was darkness in his face and a chill in his words, and something about his eyes weren't quite right, as if he were scared, but not scared like you or I would be, it was like he--"

"Like he knew something he wasn't telling you? Something horrible?" Michael asked.

"Yes!" she said. "And there was something like a shadow behind his eyes, something wild, something terrible." She paused where she stood in the kitchen doorway and her hands shook. "If there was anything he could do he said to call him straight away."

"Why didn't you?" he asked.

"There was nothing he could do," she replied. "I didn't have to be an expert to see it, what with him standing there shaking on my doorstep."

She was right, he thought. She couldn't have been more right.

"Where do you feel it most?" he asked. "Where in the house?"

"Upstairs," she said.

That's what he'd expected.

"Do you know what it is then?" she asked.

"You don't?" He looked at her hard, searching, wondering how much she knew and how much she'd forgot.

"No," she said. "The priest said only 'It' and I didn't press the matter, thought it might not be good for his health. I hoped you might tell me." She still was shaken. Her voice trembled as she spoke and her hands along with it so that her knuckles rapped twice hard on the counter when she tried to pour the tea. A third followed in the dead silence, even though she'd drawn her hands away quick as anything. Her eyes widened, her hands stock-still. "Did you hear that?" she whispered.

He nodded.

"I'm scared," she said, her face in her hands. "I'm terrified. I've never been more scared in my life."

"The tea," he said. "Is it ready?"

"Yes," she replied. She poured a cup.

He took it before she could drink it and from the pocket of his coat he took a packet of dry leaves wrapped about in plastic. He crushed a few into the cup. "Now drink it quick," he instructed. "It will calm your nerves and let you see." So she did without question.

For a moment they stayed there in the entrance hall, neither saying a word. His eyes were on the floor. There was a sound coming up through the carpet, as if someone were beneath the joists running their nails on the wood. Neither did she say anything until at last she put down the emptied cup.

"What now then?" she asked

"You must come upstairs with me," he said. "Can you do that?"

She hesitated, but consented at the last. He could see she was afraid, but there was a resolve in her too that wouldn't be coward now. He admired that.

The steps were laid in hardwood, the stairway paneled, and all the upstairs of the house was hardwood also. Their footsteps weren't silent. Each one echoed through the house and lasted into his memory. The railing was worn from countless years of use, and it even hung a bit, in need of a screw or two for repair. The landing was cold, much colder than it ought to be, as if there was a window open on some winter hell. And he could feel them watching him and hear the grate of their claws on the back of the panel board, their breath like wind in the night. It smelled like an old and empty house – and something else, something stale and foul, rotten as a corpse. With every step their eyes grew brighter, and then came the knock as of hard knuckles on the back of the panel board again, only just behind the wall in front of them.

She shivered an uncontrollable shake that went all through her body.

"Are you alright?" he asked.

And she was, though her face had gone pale and her hands wouldn't stop trembling. "I can feel them," she said. "I can feel them close."

"Don't scream," he replied. He was watching her carefully, watching her beautiful face and her kind, horrified smile. "Whatever happens, don't scream."

The hallway was cold, the rooms were empty. None had dared enter there for some time, he thought, much longer than she supposed. "How long?" he asked her again as they stood looking down the empty corridor, his hands on the wood in hopes of feeling the vibrations they made.

"Near a weak," she said without hesitation.

How could it have been only week, he wondered, brushing away the dust from the floor? But he stopped and from his jacket he struck a light to illuminate the shadows. There ran a trail of prints over the hardwood. It went from one room to the next. Prints? What then could linger? What purpose to leave a trail?

"When was the last you came up the stairs?" he asked.

"Not since it started," said she. "Not in a week."

He searched down the hall, following the prints: two doors on the left, one on the right, the walls in paper and hung with dusty old photographs: and another door at the end. There the prints in the dust vanished. It seemed an awfully big house now, a house of many secrets.

"How many rooms upstairs?" he asked.

She replied, "Three: two on the left, one on the right."

"And at the end of the hall?" he asked.

"Just three," she said.

Then what had made its home there and hidden itself beneath her eyes? What time had it stolen? What shadows hid themselves to torment her memory? He wouldn't admit it, though he was certain now. In the hall he waited in silence and thought, and then he said, "Look." He put his hands on the sides of her head and directed her eyes to that final door and wouldn't let her look away, though she struggled and choked on the tears that coursed her face. "What's there?" he demanded. "What do you see?"

"A door," she replied, and her skin went cold and her words hollow – hollow as the empty shadows of that place.

"And how long?" he asked for the third time.

"Twelve years," she replied with certainty.

"Then listen to me now," he said in earnest. He could feel it watching, growing, the shadows ever darker. "You must be strong. You must be brave. I cannot face this thing alone. It torments you, it has stolen your soul, and it is you that must face it first."

She nodded: she understood. He took her by the arm and they went in at the door. It creaked on rusted hinges. Within there was only darkness that surrounded. He could feel it on him and her hand in his. She wouldn't let go. She clutched tighter, and then her voice was in the dark though he hadn't expected it: "I don't fear you," she said, her words shaken and weak but getting stronger. "This place is my own, this darkness mine too. And what invitation you've received is mine to retake."

But it only screamed at her in reply and it grew in the shadows around them like a heavy smoke. It pressed in until he could feel its touch on his shoulder, and its breath was hot on his neck. It called to him, its voice as wretched as the very foul stench of its thought. "This woman I know, and I also know Him by name. And the Great One has spawned in this place the fear and wretched hatred that is mine. But by the Shadow, who are you?"

He didn't reply. What purpose would it serve? To her he said, "Stand close and don't wander. And cover your face. Be strong, and when it speaks to you tell it to leave. Tell it and *believe* it." He struck a light again. In the darkness it burned in gold, and he could see It, the demon, shadowed and terrible, waiting for him to speak. But he regarded it indifferently.

"Get out of my house!" she cried suddenly. Her words were strong, confident. But she was just one against him, and he was the stronger. She needed an ally. So he said, "There is no longer fear here. What service you offer is needed no more. Be gone!"

"Fear?" it scoffed. "Do you not smell it, oh wretched one? I smell it on you, I smell it on her, that putrid stench, that rotten filth of humanity. And I hunger, oh how I hunger for this ravish! In the darkness I'll take her. I'll have my way. I'll beat her, I'll rape her, and she'll know pain, she'll know fear. She'll beg for death before I'm done!" In the dark it touched her, its wicked claws on her skin and its teeth in her flesh until her blood sparkled in the light of the flame. But she didn't scream or cry; she didn't say a word.

"She doesn't fear you," he replied. "Fear is to tremble, fear is to cower. She stands tall, and she might not know what you are but I do. As she has said, you aren't welcome here anymore. Leave while you may!"

"By what power?" it demanded, and it fell on him, its horrid eyes glowering, its claws gripping his fresh. It tore at him, raging in hatred and anger, wings unfeld to rise in the darkness – such a wretched thing.

"Power?" he asked. "What power is given, what power is taken?" For only a moment he paused, his eyes on it, its eyes on him. "By the Light, in nomine Patris, et Filii, et Spiritus Sancti. Until the dawn!" The flame rose ever higher until it touched the ceiling. The shadows were removed, the room enveloped in light, and the enemy was laid bare. Amidst the dust it cowered, writhing in agony. Its bony scaled limbs rasped against the wood and its wings raked at the walls. It beseeched him with its smoldering eyes, but he sooner would've cut them out than let it stay. And then it cried with a voice like nothing that lives – the voice of the damned. "Damn you to hell, Michael!" it screamed. "What power!"

"What power indeed," answered Michael. The flame died away and the room was cast once more in darkness.

He loosed her and left her standing alone in the dark, her hands still covering her eyes. She didn't want to see what'd happened nor what was to come. She shook with sobs, her beautiful face stricken in terror. It must be undone, he thought, if not for her then for Nikki. It must be done.

He fell on the demon, its throat in his hands. Its skin was as acid, as a fire that cannot be quenched. And yet he held on as if no other could make him to let go, always tightening, always choking, always wringing the flesh. It tore at him, it writhed, it cursed, it screamed, it begged to be let go. It pleaded that he might spare it such fate. And still he held on. It'd had its chance: it chose to stay.

The floorboards beneath his feet grew hot as if a fire now burned below. Through their cracks the heat rose, and flames licked up about his knees. It was hot as a smelter. It was terrible and wretched, that place he'd been before but only once, into that dark, abysmal depth. As the dusty hardwood fell away and he hung only just above the chasm, it still in his hands, it spoke:

"It is you who should be with me there," it said. "You know this. All you must do is let go."

How he wanted to let go. It was so easy, and then he would fall to what depths awaited. Again he'd look on the flame and the fire and the great and mighty citadel at the end of the worlds. Part of him missed it. Another part of him felt guilty. He should be with them, the ones who suffered. He longed it might be so, that he might know the punishment for his guilt.

"Michael!" she cried, and she was by his side, taking his arm and pulling him away. The hardwood was beneath him again, the dust on his hands. The room was in darkness – though not as dark as it once had been. Not so terribly cold either. He laid there, the air in his lungs cool and refreshing, and the sweat was on his face, that fire still burning in his eyes. All he had to do was let go.

But she had held him back.

"What was that?" she asked, her eyes wild with question, with wonder. "What happened? I saw you standing over an abyss and I thought you were going to jump!"

"It doesn't matter. It's gone," said he. "You're free."

ABOUT THE AUTHOR

AD Bane is an avid enthusiast of science-fiction and fantasy. He's been dreaming and writing both since he first began to learn the art as a boy. He especially enjoys tales that stretch the confines of their genres and imagination.

AD Bane also enjoys philosophy and is fascinated by the machinery of the human condition. He writes stories such as this one both for pleasure and to present ideas that he believes can be difficult to grasp in reality. He's written many short stories, one novel, and is working on more, including a direct sequel to his first printed novel, Beyond the Wasteland.

You can find all his work available at Amazon, or visit ADBane.com to see what he's working on next.

BEYOND THE WASTELAND

A novel
By AD Bane

"It came from the east and went into the west with a rustle of the prairie grass and a cry of the rails that lasted on the wind, even until it was well beyond the next hill."

"It was a demon-train, Tucker, an evil thing if ever I saw one . . . and I intend to catch it."

Paperback and e-book now available at Amazon.ca and Amazon.com!

www.ingramcontent.com/pod-product-compliance
Lightning Source LLC
Chambersburg PA
CBHW020609130626
46552CB00007B/3115